Phoenix Young Readers Library

The Tales of Wamugumo

Phoenix Young Readers Library

1. The Valley of the Dead — Akberali Manji
2. The Battle of Mogori — Zaccheaus arap Kimeto
3. The Tales of Wamugumo — P.N. Kuguru
4. Mzee Nyachote — Roeland Japuonjo
5. The Proud Ostrich — J.K. Njoroge
6. The Greedy Host — J.K. Njoroge
7. The Fly Whisk — Stephen Gichuru
8. The Orange Thieves — Charity Dahal
9. The Magic Stone — J. Ibongia & L. Dobrin
10. Onyango's Triumph — Leo Odera Omolo
11. Beautiful Nyakio — Fredrick Ndung'u
12. The Children of the Forest — Joel Makumi
13. The Girl Who Couldn't Keep a Secret — Clare Omanga
14. Give the Devil his Due — W.K. Boruett
15. Njogu the Prophet — Jamlick Mutua
16. The Adventures of Thiga — C.M. Mureithi
17. The Coconut Girl — Joseph Kabui
18. Wake Up and Open Your Eyes — Edward Muhire
19. The River Without Frogs — Writers' Committee
20. Travels of a Raindrop — David Ng'osos
21. Lots of Wonders — Sam Mbure
22. The Great Siege of Fort Jesus — Valerie Cuthbert
23. Pamela the Probation Officer — Cynthia Hunter
24. Truphena Student Nurse — Cynthia Hunter
25. Truphena City Nurse — Cynthia Hunter
26. Anna the Air Hostess — Cynthia Hunter
27. Captured by Raiders — Benjamin S. Wegesa
28. The Circle of Revenge — David Mwaurah
29. The Town Tricksters — David Mwaurah
30. Njaga the Town Monkey — Joel Makumi
31. End of the Beginning — Joel Makumi
32. The Cruel Burden — Okoth Gonza
33. The Tumbling of the Tumbulu — Liselotte Christensen
34. Jessicah — Patricia Farrell

and more .... many more

The Tales of Wamugumo

and other stories

PETER KUGURU

Illustrations: Adrienne Moore

 PHOENIX PUBLISHERS, NAIROBI

First published in 1968
This edition published in 1988 by
Phoenix Publishers Ltd.,
22 Kijabe Street,
P.O.Box 30474-00100,
Nairobi, Kenya.

© Text: Peter Ngibuini Kuguru, 1968,1987
© Illustrations: Phoenix Publishers Ltd.

ISBN 9966 47 055 7

Reprinted in 1988,1989,1990,1991,1993,1996,1998, 2001, 2002, 2005, 2006, 2007, 2010, 2011, 2013, 2014, 2019

Printed by:
Modern Lithographic (K) Limited
P.O. Box 52810 - 00200,
Nairobi,
Kenya.

Contents

1. Meet Wamugumo 1
2. The squirrel, the leopard and the hyena 7
3. Why the antelope is always impatient 15
4. Wanjacia, the half man 18
5. The foolish woman 24
6. Unblessed marriage 27
7. The cruel man died 34
8. Why the hen will never tolerate the hawk 42
9. Why the partridge drinks only dew 45
10. The foolish Lion and Hare 47
11. Cinji, Kamau and Mwari 54
12. Kahuru the crow 62
13. The last days of Wamugumo 66

1

Meet Wamugumo

Wamugumo was a famous Kikuyu character. He died only a few years ago. His home was in Nyeri, and he came from poor parents. His father died when he was still young and he lived with his mother.

Many people become famous because of their riches, wisdom, talents or something which the common man does not possess. However, the things that made Wamugumo outstanding were rather ridiculous.

He possessed a remarkable appetite. Wamugumo was fed by various people in the course of his life. But when these kind people saw how much he ate, they deserted him and did not give him food anymore. They realized that their stores would not be enough for them and Wamugumo.

His heavy eating undoubtedly contributed to his size. He was about seven feet tall. He was not fat but he was very strong. Indeed he was stronger than anyone else in the country.

Because his mother was unable to feed him he had to leave home to look for work. He was employed by a farmer who gave him a bag of maize flour every two days. He also hunted buck to go with the flour, and his employer brought him meat from any wild animals he shot.

Wamugumo had to pay for his meals. When he accompanied his employer and the car got stuck somewhere, no outside help was needed. Not only could Wamugumo easily lift a car, but he also only needed a tiny shove for him to push it right over.

If you had never seen Wamugumo work you wouldn't have believed a man could do the work he did. He could dig an acre of ground in one day. This amazed his employer. Indeed at first the farmer even sent someone to make sure that Wamugumo was not being helped by angels.

As the years passed, Wamugumo grew so gigantic that his employer feared that one day he might become hostile and dangerous. So Wamugumo was sent home. At that time, the country people were beginning to adopt modern farming. Since they wanted work done quickly and cheaply, they joined together in large groups. They would all go together to one man's home where they would dig and prepare his shamba for two or three days. The owner of the land would give food for free. Then everyone would go to the next man's and then the next, until everyone in the group had had a chance of getting two days' work done.

Wamugumo knew all about this and he realized that it was one way of surviving. To a man who needed help he would say, "I have got a group coming to my shamba but my shamba is already cleared. If you can afford to feed the group, I will let you have them for nothing."

On the day appointed for the group to come Wamugumo would appear carrying ten *pangas* and would be shown the place to be cleared. Then he would say that the group were on their way. If only the shamba owner would leave and not worry himself, Wamugumo would supervise them and see that everything went properly.

When the owner left, Wamugumo would begin to clear the land, working as hard as he could. Wamugumo never got exhausted. He could work the whole morning without stopping. He did not stop until he was satisfied that he had cleared a piece as large as ten people could clear in a morning. Then he planted the ten pangas in a row along the edge of the cleared area.

Wamugumo left the shamba and told the owner, "The group is already hungry. They have gone to the river for a quick bath. In the meantime, would you please bring the food?" The owner was surprised at the amount of work done, and done so well. After bringing the food, the shamba owner left Wamugumo waiting for the group to come back from the river.

Wamugumo set about eating the food. He swallowed and gulped piece after piece until all the food, enough for eleven people, was finished. After lunch he again worked tirelessly and then, before going home, asked for more food for the group. He would then eat all of this too.

Besides eating, Wamugumo loved fighting. No one could survive even a light blow from Wamugumo's fist. This was about the size of a large loaf of bread. When Wamugumo wanted to fight he went alone with his spear to the forest and hunted animals.

The game scouts did not harass him for this. They may even at times have mistaken him for an animal himself. He never shaved or had his hair cut. He wore only the hairy skins of animals. But perhaps the scouts never asked him about his hunting for another obvious reason — questions might mean losing teeth.

Wamugumo was also famous for banana hunting. When Wamugumo grew hungry, he sometimes walked into someone's shamba and uprooted a banana tree. After uprooting the whole plant Wamugumo took it to a place in the forest which he had cleared. All round the clearing were leafy poles and supporting twigs, providing a shelter. Wamugumo dug a hole between the supporting poles and replanted the banana tree. The banana fruits faced inside. Then Wamugumo would build a fire inside and roast all the bananas and eat them. After the rains, Wamugumo's forest house was strongly supported by flourishing banana plants.

Wamugumo also had the power to see into the future and most of his prophecies turned out to be true. He would tell a man how many children he had at home, and whether or not he would be wealthy. It must be admitted that Wamugumo sometimes took advantage of his powers.

He told most of the enquirers that they would become wealthy. He would tell boys that they would have many wives and children, and that they would be happy. In return, the children fetched firewood and water for Wamugumo. They ran for fire from neighbours' houses.

Children loved Wamugumo and they were constantly with him wherever he went. He would never touch money, he said. Whenever he was given money he gave it to the children. The children then went to buy bananas or food for him. In return, he told the children exciting stories and they enjoyed his company. This book contains the stories he told.

2

The squirrel, the leopard and the hyena

The squirrel is well known for his wisdom and cunning. He has many times behaved like a rogue. The other animals are always angry with the squirrel and the squirrel is always quarrelling with them.

But long ago, the squirrel was a great friend of the leopard. They used to walk together and go to dances. One day, the two were asked to a wedding party. The bride was the cousin of the leopard and so he was due a share of the dowry.

At the party they ate meat until they could eat no more. Then the leopard was given his share of the dowry. He was given a large herd of cattle and a few goats. He was kind and so he decided that the herd should be divided between himself and his good friend, the squirrel. The two had a long way to travel before reaching home and it was already late in the evening. But they decided to start on their journey.

When they had travelled a good distance they became so tired that they had to rest. The leopard became worried that they might lose the herd if they went to sleep. They decided that one would sleep, while the other was on the look out. The squirrel volunteered to sleep first. The leopard kept a keen watch on the herd and there was no trouble. When he had done enough sentry duty he called the squirrel from his sleep so that they could exchange places.

When the squirrel was quite sure that the leopard was in a deep sleep, he went to the herd of cattle and cut all their tails off. He led the animals away into the bush and left them there. Then very quickly he dug holes all over the clearing, and put the tails in each hole so that the bushy end remained facing the sky.

When all the tails were well in the ground, with the hairy ends facing the sky, the squirrel shouted from place to place as if he was mad, crying and cursing. This awakened the leopard. The leopard did not know what was going on and when he awoke from his sleep, he listened and heard the squirrel shouting madly, "Wake up, Leopard, wake up, wake up! The cows are being swallowed by the earth! Come and help! Come and pull!!"

Looking at the squirrel, the leopard saw him tugging the tails. He went from one tail to another but he was not successful. The leopard jumped up and ran to the tails. He and the squirrel pulled and pulled. When a tail came off, the squirrel said, "We pulled too hard and fiercely, I think. That's why the tail came off the cow."

They pulled out most of the tails until they were so exhausted that they gave up. The squirrel started crying. In the morning they went home. When the leopard had gone to his house, the squirrel ran back to the scene of the disaster. He found that the cattle were safe. He drove them to his uncle's home and told him the secret.

After many years, the leopard had forgotten the incident. The squirrel was aware of this. He went to his uncle and asked for his cattle. He gave his uncle the young calves for keeping the herd. He brought the herd home with him. He did not let the leopard come into his company again because he knew that the leopard would recognise the herd immediately.

The leopard heard, by a rumour going round the countryside, that the squirrel had a large herd. The leopard wanted to see this herd but the squirrel would not let him. So he decided to wait until he had a chance. At that time, the squirrel used to slaughter a cow every evening and invite the leopard to come and eat the meat. The squirrel insisted, however, that he should only come at night when it was dark.

One day, the squirrel was careless. He had asked his neighbours to come to a drinking party. He had meant to send the animals away before daylight so that they would not see his stolen cattle. The guests were so drunk that they had to stay till the next day. But the leopard had drunk very little and the next morning he saw the herd. He recognised all the cattle since none of them had any tails. He went to ask the squirrel about these strange cows.

The squirrel tried to put the matter off, but it was no good. He had been found out. He was told that his punishment would be death. Since the squirrel had once deceived the vulture during a meat-party, the vulture supported the leopard. The two decided that they would kill and eat the squirrel. When the squirrel heard of the plot, he ran away. He ran very much faster than the leopard but the vulture spotted him from above. The squirrel raced down a hole.

When the leopard arrived at the hole, he found the vulture waiting. He told him to wait there and make sure that the squirrel did not escape while he, the leopard, went to fetch firewood and fire so that they could smoke the squirrel out of the hole. The squirrel heard the plan. He waited until the leopard was gone.

Then he came out of the hole with a handful of soil. He said to the vulture, "If I were you on guard, I would open my eyes wide so that the prisoner would see that I am watching him, and he wouldn't try to escape." The vulture opened his eyes and immediately the squirrel threw the soil at his face. Some of the soil went into the vulture's eyes and the squirrel ran away.

When the leopard came back, he found the vulture half-blind and crying. The vulture narrated what had happened. The leopard told him to go and find the squirrel within a certain number of days. Otherwise the vulture would lose his own blood.

The vulture worked hard, and in a few days he spotted the squirrel. He told the leopard, and together they managed to capture the squirrel and bring him home.

The squirrel begged them to spare him, and said that if they did, he would become the leopard's slave for ever. The leopard found this quite a pleasing idea and agreed to it.

The leopard gave orders that every evening, when he came home, he wanted to find meat ready cooked. He told the squirrel to sit on a bed with the meat and throw pieces to him sitting underneath, until he was satisfied. Failure to do this would mean death to the squirrel.

The squirrel did his duty well. One day he decided that he would take revenge. He had been ordered to call the leopard 'Father'. This did not please him.

The squirrel went into the garden and found a large stone. When he was roasting meat, he placed the stone on the fire under the meat so that fat from the meat would drip onto the stone. The stone became red hot.

When the leopard came home, he sat in his usual place for meat. The squirrel also went to his usual place from where he threw pieces of meat to the leopard who swallowed them. Then he threw the red hot stone. The leopard swallowed this also. His insides were terribly burned. He tried to vomit the stone, but it was no good. He jumped about in pain, moaning and groaning, but there was no chance of getting the stone out and eventually he died.

The squirrel was not displeased, neither was he sorry. He hid his 'Father' behind the door. Later that evening, the hyena came for fire. He feared the leopard very much so he asked for fire from outside. The squirrel whispered to him, "Father is asleep. Come in and have some meat but come very quietly. Don't wake him."

The hyena thought that was quite a nice idea and did not hesitate. He was shown the meat, just in front of the door, and was told to eat slowly. While the hyena was eating cautiously, the squirrel tied the tail of the hyena to the tail of the leopard. When the knot was quite tight, the squirrel opened the door wide. Then he called, tapping the leopard, "Father, Father, wake up! The hyena is eating your meat ! Do you hear?"

When the hyena heard this, he shot out of the house. He turned, and behind him saw the leopard. He increased his speed and in doing so dragged the leopard with him. Whenever he turned round he saw the leopard and ran even faster. The squirrel jumped on the house and cried, "Father, I bet you will catch him. Hyena, I bet you are too fast to be caught."

This encouraged the hyena. At last the tail of the leopard came off and as the hyena was moving very fast, he jerked forward and fell down so that his forefeet were broken. He went home limping. When his forefeet had healed he discovered that they were shorter than the back feet.

All the leopard family heard the story. They thought both the squirrel and the hyena were to blame, so they decided that both should be killed.

When he heard his, the hyena fled off into the bush and hid by the river. The squirrel climbed a tree which was so thin that if any of the leopard family tried to pursue him the tree would break. The squirrel could easily leap to a nearby tree but a leopard would fall to the ground.

The cunning of the squirrel so infuriated the leopards that even today they look for squirrels. The hyena never comes out during the day. He sleeps when it is light and only leaves his home at night, in case he should ever meet a leopard!

3

Why the antelope is always impatient

Once upon a time, women ruled men in all ways. Everything was the other way round from what it is today. Men were worked like slaves and were beaten. They had to salute whenever a woman said an angry word. The goats at that time were wild and women used to rear bucks and antelopes.

One day, because of women's tyrannical rule, men became angry. All of a sudden, without warning, the men unanimously took sticks and clubs and started on the women. The women did not know what was going on but they had to accept that the world was against them. They were taken by surprise, beaten and chased all over the gardens and fields. As a result, the women's kingdom fell. The bucks fled and became wild and men tamed the previously wild goats and cows. Since then women have been under men.

Before the men could settle down completely, a number of things happened. Rumours started to run up and down the countryside that fire was coming to finish the world. The only thing to do was to dig big holes and hide in them. This was all right for the human beings but what about the animals? They would not be able to go into holes because of their long horns. All the animals had very long curving horns, like those of an antelope.

While the women were digging caves to hide in, men called for all animals that did not want to burn to come and get their horns shortened or removed.

The first day, the elephant, the hare, the antelope, the hyena and the rat came. The elephant was first. While the men were working on him the antelope moved further back, frightened by what he saw. The same thing happened each time the antelope watched another animal getting his horns shortened. All the animals present on the first day had their horns either removed or shortened but the antelope refused, saying that he would come the following day.

For many days the animals came. The antelope was present on every occasion but due to his cowardice he never got his horns shortened. He kept on saying, "Tomorrow, I will get my horns removed."

Day after day he came but his tomorrow stayed tomorrow.

One day, before the rains, the full moon shone fiercely on the horizon. To every animal it looked as if the long-expected fire had come at last and all the animals disappeared into their holes. The antelope went from one hole to another but he could not fit into any of them. His horns were too long. He was seen rushing at high speed towards the man's cave and desperately shouting, "Man, man, man, come and cut my horns, come and cut my horns!"

But the man did not want to come out and burn, so he shouted from within, "Go away, I have told you many a time. You should always be prepared if any danger is anticipated."

Since the fire appeared to come from the east, the antelope started running west. He ran for a whole night. When day came the fire disappeared.

After a short rest, the antelope started eating but after each swallow he looked round on all sides to make sure that fire was not coming. From that time till now, the antelope is always worried about fire, so after every gulp of food that he takes, he turns to all sides, glancing at the horizons to make sure that there is no danger of fire.

4

Wanjacia, the half man

Githiru is a very old village situated near Chania river. Up Chania river is a very dense forest where men go hunting and women go to fetch firewood.

Once long ago in Githiru village there lived three brothers. They went hunting together and they ate whatever they caught. They never went very deep into the forest. Inside the forest, it was dark and everyone was afraid to penetrate it. If the three brothers followed a beast and it went right into the forest they left it and looked for another.

One day they looked for a beast but could find none. They beat all the bushes but no animals came out of cover. In the afternoon, tired and exhausted, they decided to leave for home. Just as they were leaving, a large antelope jumped from a nearby bush. They pursued it. It leaped over the bushes but they still toiled on. They followed and followed until eventually the antelope entered the deep forest and disappeared into the dark shadows.

The three men had no hope of finding another quarry, so they decided to keep chasing this one, even though it had gone into the terrible forest. They followed the antelope for many hours by its footmarks. When they were in almost complete darkness, they met a figure of a man that was most strange. He was one sided, with one hand, one foot, one leg, one eye, one nose, half a head and half a body. They could not bear such a horrifying sight. They tried to run but found it was dark on all sides.

The half man told the three brothers that his name was Wanjacia. He said that this was his kingdom. He told the three brothers that since they had trespassed without permission, they would never leave it again, as a punishment. They explained that they would give Wanjacia any suitable rewards if they were allowed to go home.

Wanjacia sympathised with them and said they could leave if they were prepared to take an oath and swear that they would never tell anyone that they had seen a half man. The three brothers readily promised. They were shown the hiding place of the panting antelope and they killed and carried it home. Before they were escorted to the forest edge, they also had to promise never to return again. Then they were shown the way out.

When they went home, they found that three days had elapsed. They were asked to explain why they had taken so long and had caught only one beast. They refused to explain. Eventually, their grandmother took aside the youngest of the three brothers. She tried to persuade him with soothing tones but he refused to tell. The grandmother tried again to get the information. The boy was angered by his grandmother's insistence. He told her that he certainly would not tell her then and she must stop asking him. She asked when he would tell her. He said he would tell her later, perhaps in a year's time.

Many years elapsed. One day, the grandmother remembered the boy's promise. She asked him. He told her all about Wanjacia, because he thought that Wanjacia must have died by then.

The three brothers used to sleep in the same bed. The youngest one slept between the other two because he occupied the least space. The night after he had related the story of Wanjacia to his grandmother, Wanjacia came and cut the boy in two halves lengthwise, very neatly. Blood filled the bed. The two brothers heard blood dripping on the floor but they thought that someone had wet the bed during a dream.

In the morning the two elder brothers found out the truth. Their younger brother looked like two Wanjacias. They perceived that he must have told someone about the half man.

The two sides of the younger brother were taken and thrown away into the bushes. They thought the matter was ended. But the following night, the sleepers heard a high-pitched voice singing:

Wanjacia, Wanjacia Kamanandi!
You have carried me on your back
With threads from the Miaritha bark!
Eh huu, a heavy load ! Help me ho!

After the song, they heard something heavy fall on the ground. They did not hear any more and so they dozed off and slept till morning. In the morning, outside the house they found the two sides of the youngest brother who had been thrown away the day before. As previously, they each took a part and carried it into the bush.

The following night they heard the song exactly as it had been sung the night before. They knew what had happened but they were afraid to go out and see. The following morning they found the two parts of the body again lying by the house. This time the brothers took the body further than before, buried it in a hole and placed large logs of heavy wood and huge boulders on top. The following night, the same song was heard and the following morning the pieces of body were again outside.

This time something had to be done. They threw away the two pieces and decided to stay awake at night so as to see what could be done to the unfortunate Wanjacia. That night, the strange figure of Wanjacia was seen carrying a heavy load. Before he could start singing, he was greeted by the brothers. He was asked what he would accept to stop bringing back the dead body.

Wanjacia refused any presents or payment saying that as he had done this once before he was not going to make the same mistake again. The brothers continued to urge him. Finally he accepted a few goats and a gourd of fat and said that the boy would live with him in the forest, but he would stay in two parts. The boy was brought back to life and the three half men walked away, into the dark forest.

Throughout their lives the remaining two brothers never told anyone about Wanjacia. They feared the half man and did not wish the same fate as their foolish, talkative brother.

5

The foolish woman

Once long ago, the Kikuyu quarrelled with the Maasai, as they often did in those days. The Maasai used to kill any Kikuyu boys that they found and kidnap any Kikuyu woman. Whenever the women went to gather foodstuff from the shambas, they were escorted by men fighters whose only job was to fight for the tribe and protect them.

One day, the women were escorted as usual to their shamba. After they had collected enough food for the following week they were taken home.

But one foolish woman had forgotten to collect vegetables. She decided she would go to fetch the vegetables the following day. She was advised not to risk going alone as it was dangerous. Despite all the warnings she was determined to go. When she was out of sight of the village, she grew nervous. She thought what would happen if the Maasai moran came, but she did not stop. It seemed that one part of her urged her to go back and was cowardly but the other part pressed her on. By the time she reached her shamba, she wished she had not come, yet she was happy she had arrived safely.

Alone and in her heart, she debated whether she should go back or whether she should collect the vegetables. Eventually she decided to get the vegetables. Since it was in a season when plants were flowering, the shamba was full of bees buzzing from one flower to the next.

Whenever the woman stepped on a dry leaf and it rattled, she jumped back, ready to call for help. Any noise, however slight, frightened and disturbed her. She was very attentive and was conscious of any sound. She realized the danger she was in.

When she bent over a vegetable to pick it, a bee buzzed from it. She jumped back. She listened cautiously and decided that there must be danger in that part of the garden. She moved to another place which she thought was safer. As she bent to pick a vegetable, another bee buzzed from a vegetable nearby. She felt that someone somewhere must be watching her.

She was sure she was surrounded by the Maasai. She knew she had done wrong to ignore the advice of her fellow villagers. She realized that if she started for home she would not be able to get there before she was caught by the Maasai. What could she do?

"Better get on collecting vegetables," she thought. "Perhaps after all no one is after me."

So she gathered her courage and started to bend over a vegetable. Bees from nearby flowers buzzed away. She got so frightened and felt she could bear it no longer. She could not run home because she was surrounded. She started mistaking bananas for men. Once she burst out shouting for help. Things were hovering around her, she thought. She grew very impatient before the village men arrived.

When the villagers arrived, she explained that there were men all around. After a clear search not even footprints were found. The men got very angry with her, first because of the warning she had been given and had ignored, then because of asking for help when it was not needed. She would have saved the men the trouble of searching through the thick, impenetrable bushes at home. She would have stayed at home if she had collected the vegetables at the right time. "Really," they complained. "Women die through their own fault."

6

Unblessed marriage

Many years ago it was strictly forbidden for any young unmarried man to be seen anywhere with a young woman. Anyone caught would be heavily fined by the elders.

When a man thought he was old enough to marry he started looking for a good girl, not by talking to girls but by observing them. When the man chose one of the girls, the girls had no way of knowing which one he had picked. The procedure was for the man to get ready one evening when he was sure the girl he desired was at home. He wore his ceremonial dress and took his spear with him. He went straight to the girl's home.

The man planted his spear upright in front of the girl's home and waited for people to see him. The girl or girls at home are thus warned. The mother hides, the father goes to his **thingira** (small house).

The girl then has a few minutes to decide whether she wants the man or not. If she wants the man, she goes and takes the spear and plants it inside the house. If she does not want the man, she ignores him.

If there are many girls, the oldest is the one who has the right to do something about the spear. The others may not marry before the eldest. If the man waits for a long time and thinks he is ignored, he leaves and, if he is interested in that girl, he tries his luck again. If the spear is uprooted the man follows the girl. When they are in the house the man can talk to the girl. The mother then comes in and asks the girl to give the visitor some porridge. Various other ceremonies are carried out from time to time until the wedding.

One day a young exceedingly beautiful woman decided that she was too good for a man who had come to her home. His spear stood upright in front of the house. The man tried his luck once, twice and again, but he was always refused. He knew that his happiness would depend on that one girl and he passionately longed for her. He decided to trick her for he knew he must get her by any means.

He went into the bush. He uprooted all the bad smelling herbs that he could find and put them in a gourd. When they were nicely tucked in, the man waited till it was dark.

Then he went to the girl's home and hid by the side of her house. When she came out, he followed her. The girl entered her mother's house. The man hid outside the house and exposed the smelly contents of the gourd. Then he closed it and hid it. The mother became very much irritated by the stinking smell. She thought the girl was smelling.

The girl was upset and left her mother. She went to take her father some food in the **thingira**. As before, the young man uncorked the gourd and the whole **thingira** smelt like rotten eggs. The girl's father sent her away hurriedly, thinking that it was she who was smelling. She was convinced then that she was the one who smelt so bad. She decided that if that was the case, she wouldn't be welcome in any house except her grandmother's. She went there.

The young man, still following her at a short distance, made sure that she was safely inside. He stole up, opened the gourd and inserted its mouth under the door. The grandmother was shocked by the smell. She squeezed her nostrils together. She called the girl every bad word she could recall. The girl felt desperate. She left her grandmother in a hurry. She planned to go to a lonely place and weep. She did not know what to do.

When he approached the girl he pretended that he could smell something horrible.

The following morning, she took a pot and left home for the river. In the river she filled her pot and sat down to wash. The man, who was hiding in the bush admiring her, made sure no one was near, then he showed himself. When he approached the girl, he pretended that he could smell something horrible. He asked the girl what was smelling. She explained to him that, since the day before, she had been smelling like that and she did not know what to do.

The man told the girl that he could show her a cure for the smell on condition that she would marry him later. In desperation the girl accepted the offer. The man went into the bush and collected various types of leaves. He told her to scrub herself with the leaves and then wash herself, after which he would come and smell her. When she had washed, he sniffed at her and assured her that she no longer smelt.

The girl went home happily thinking that the man had really cured her of the smell. A few days later the man dressed for the ceremony, and carrying his spear, appeared in the girl's home. His spear was taken by the girl the minute he planted it. The girl's parents wondered why their well known beautiful daughter should accept such an ugly man but they had no objection. It was for the girl to decide. After this event, the families proceeded to arrange a wedding ceremony and party.

Everything was successful and the beautiful girl who had refused many handsome men was now married to a poor, ugly man.

The married couple stayed together for many years. They got a home and children. One day, while the man was in his **thingira** his wife came to bring food. He told her that he wished to tell her something special. She sat near him and listened to the story of how she had been tricked into marrying. The wife became very angry. She wept the whole night at the thought that had it not been her husband's cunning trick, she would have married a handsome, rich man who could have made her many times happier. She wept the whole morning. She was ashamed that she had been foolish enough to let herself be fooled and angry at him for being so sly.

She spent many hours thinking of what to do with herself. She was too old to marry again or to go to her home and she had children whom she dearly loved. She decided to remain in her husband's home for their sake. But she did not want to see her husband. She refused to talk to him or serve him food.

After several days, however, she had a change of heart. Her husband had been very tactful with her during this time and she realized that he had been kind and generous during their life together. One morning she got up early, cooked some food and brought it to her husband.

They were very happy for the rest of their days. Then the husband knew that he had turned a useless proud girl into a good wife.

7

The cruel man died

Once upon a time, there lived a man who had two wives. He loved the younger wife whose name was Nyende. The older wife called Mukuru was treated badly. She worked hard but she was given only a little to eat. She had only one daughter, a charming girl who was not as nicely clothed as Nyende's children.

Mukuru's daughter, Wanjiru, grew up well. She was loved by all the neighbours. She was helpful and her smile attracted everyone. She was very kind. She loved her mother, and she helped her a great deal.

As time passed, Mukuru became weaker and weaker, and eventually became really sick. She stayed in bed for many days. No one but Wanjiru looked after her. Then Mukuru died and was buried by the people of her clan.

Wanjiru was left alone and sorrowful. She wept for many days. She tried to cope with the people at home, her half-sisters and brothers, but she was too sorrowful to play. Now Mukuru was dead she was even more badly treated by her father. She could not bear to stay in such an atmosphere.

One evening, she ran away from home and went to the shamba. That night she slept under the leaves of a pumpkin vine. Very early in the morning, she heard monkeys laughing and shuffling about above her. She woke up and went to where the monkeys were. She was greeted by the monkeys happily. The monkeys gave her their food and she stayed with them.

The father became very angry about Wanjiru. He found out where she had gone. One evening, he hid near the pumpkin vine. He had a long sheath which contained a newly sharpened *panga*. He also had a spear and some arrows. Wanjiru left the monkeys and went to where she used to sleep under the pumpkin vine. As she approached, her father saw her. He unsheathed his *panga*. Wanjiru drew nearer to her father. When she reached him, he struck her head with the *panga* and Wanjiru fell dead. Her father went home.

No one knew what had happened. Some days later, Nyende's children went into the garden to pick vegetables. They were surprised to see Wanjiru's body lying there near the pumpkin vine. They ran away and went to report to their parents. It was a surprise to Nyende but of course the father knew all about it. Little was said about Wanjiru. She was soon forgotten. However, she was remembered, when her cousin (Mukuru's sister's daughter) came to stay with the children of Nyende.

Wanjiru's body decayed away leaving only bones. Rain fell and the sun shone. Many months passed. The monkeys never forgot Wanjiru. They travelled to far places to find a prophet who could come and bring Wanjiru to life again. Eventually, in a distant country they found Mugo, the dove, who was well known because of his magical powers.

They told Mugo about Wanjiru. He said he would bring her to life on condition that they paid him well. The monkeys did not have money or property. They thought and thought. They knew no place where they could steal the required amount of property. Mugo, the magician, decided that if they could not pay him, he would raise her from death, and then she would live with him. This was agreed.

When Mugo arrived at the place where Wanjiru had been killed he realized that he was late and needed to use very special powers. There was no body, only bones. He joined all the bones together.

He did some magic and turned the soil which had previously been Wanjiru's body, into muscles again. He shaped a very graceful and agreeable body on the bones. Wanjiru looked so beautiful that she seemed fit to be a princess.

Mugo took her to the land where he lived. He bored a hole in Wanjiru's head. He put in a soul and plugged the hole with a feather from his tail. From that moment, Wanjiru came alive and resumed her previous helpfulness. She travelled to the river every day to meet her half-sisters and her cousin. They came for water every morning. Wanjiru saw them but did not talk to them. She hid by the river plants.

The children started to dislike their step cousin. One day they went to get water from the river with heavy water pots. When they had filled the water pots, each child helped the other to lift a water pot to the head. They helped each other but not one of them helped Wanjiru's cousin. She sat down, desolate. She could not lift a full pot by herself, but if she went home with a pot half full, she would be told to go back for some more.

She wondered what she could do. She waited for someone to pass by, but no-one came and she started crying. She thought of all her friends who were far away, her own sisters and relatives. Then she said, "If Wanjiru was here, she would help me."

Just then she heard a voice from the bushes, "I am here and I will help you." Wanjiru emerged from the bushes and the two girls ran towards each other. At first, they both wept. Then Wanjiru helped her cousin, and went down the river to her new house while her cousin went home.

Wanjiru's cousin narrated everything that had happened to the family. She was beaten and told not to bring back dead memories. No one believed her but she did not mind.

Whenever she went to the river she met Wanjiru. She told the family but she was scorned and mocked for no one believed her. One day the other children hid near the river to test their cousin's story. They saw Wanjiru. They ran home quickly and told their parents what they had seen. Now the children were believed.

The father and mother decided to go and see Wanjiru for themselves. The father was ashamed, and feared it really might be Wanjiru, whom he had murdered. The two hid by the river when the children filled their pots. They helped each other, leaving Wanjiru's cousin alone. Then Wanjiru's cousin whispered and Wanjiru came out very gracefully. Nyende and her husband ran to meet Wanjiru, and said that she must come home with them. She said she could not do so. They urged her but she refused. Eventually, they took her with them by force.

Mugo wondered why Wanjiru did not come home that night. He had told her that failure to come home at any time would mean death. Mugo knew that Wanjiru would now have to die, because once he had said something it had to be obeyed. Also, whoever had brought about Wanjiru's death had to die.

Mugo discovered that Wanjiru had been taken home by her father. So Mugo went to Wanjiru's home. He found Wanjiru sitting outside the house guarded by her father. Mugo flew round them a number of times, then he sang:

Give me back my feather
So I can go home into the forest
Where rain has fallen
Where the sun has shone and trees have
 grown high.
Give me back my feather.

Then Mugo the dove flew away. They watched him. Sometimes he came very near. The father tried to kill him but was unsuccessful. Then he sat down and sang again. He tried many times to snatch away the feather from Wanjiru's head and though Wanjiru's father was usually quick enough to protect her, Mugo eventually managed to snatch the feather away. The

Wanjiru's father was usually quick enough protect her.

soul escaped from Wanjiru's body and she died. All her muscles crumbled away into soil leaving only the bones.

Mugo flew home happily. Wanjiru's father was very moved by what had happened. As he had brought about Wanjiru's death, he too must die. While he was still confused, he unsheathed his *panga* and killed himself. Nyende did not die then but she was worn out by cares and worries. She was haunted by both Wanjiru's and her husband's ghosts. She lived very sorrowfully, and eventually she also died leaving her home to her children. Wanjiru's cousin went to her own home where she lived happily throughout her life.

8

Why the hen will never tolerate the hawk

In the old days, Mrs. Hen and Mrs. Hawk were great friends. They used to visit one another. They often loaned their goods to one another. In short they had many things in common.

One day Mrs. Hen and Mrs. Hawk went out together to hunt mice. They both perched on high ground overlooking the mice's house. They aimed their arrows at the front door and waited patiently for their quarry to appear. Soon Mrs. Hen saw a mouse appearing. She aimed, shot and missed. The mouse went into the house quickly and informed the other mice and so, that day, the two hunters went home empty-handed. This did not please Mrs. Hawk.

A few weeks later, the two were called to a wedding party, held by Mr. Rabbit. After the ceremonies there was dancing. Mr. and Mrs. Hawk were not as well treated as Mr. and Mrs. Hen. The Hawks were not pretty to look at, of course, but Mr. and Mrs. Hen were.

This made the Hawks envious and they decided to kill the Hens on their way home.

Going home from the party, the Hens were very happy. The Hawks were quiet and conspiratory. The Hawks could not decide where to carry out their plan or how. Eventually, the two families parted. The following morning Mrs. Hen sent her child to go and borrow a hoe from Mrs. Hawk. The child was sent away empty-handed by Mrs. Hawk with a message that ran as follows:

"Diplomatic relations have been broken between you and us for reasons best known to yourself, one of them being that you can't hunt."

Mr. and Mrs. Hawk sent back all the things they had borrowed from the Hens and demanded their own things. The Hens packed all the goods that belonged to the Hawks and sent them back. Although the Hawks knew that all their things had been sent, they claimed that one item was missing. "And could it be sent here immediately."

The Hens were not sure. They scratched all the ground around their house but could not find the 'missing item'. Eventually they sent one of their children to report that the 'missing item' was nowhere to be found. The Hawks caught the Hens' child, cooked it and ate it. They reported that they were going to eat all the Hen's children if the 'missing item' was not found. The Hens laboriously scratched the ground over and over again. They never found it.

The Hawks set out to capture all the Hens' children but the Hens hid their children. From that time all the Hens hide whenever they see a Hawk and all the Hawks hunt for the Hens' children. Even today the Hens scratch the ground to find the Hawks' 'missing item.'

9

Why the partridge drinks only dew

When the partridge boy was still very young, he ran away from home and went to town. He had no food to eat and he had nowhere to sleep. He became very unhealthy and dirty, like any other town boy. Any food he ate, he had to steal. He became such a bad boy that he was noted by everyone. Everywhere he went, the people knew him and were aware of him. He was eventually reported by the townspeople to the Mayor. The boy was sent home in disgrace.

At home, the boy was a great nuisance. He was very disobedient and he mistreated the other children. He refused to do any work, and so he was beaten. He ran away from home again and went to stay with his grandmother. She did not mind him much. So they stayed together.

When the grandmother became too old to do much work, she needed his help. He was a big boy by then, but he would not help his grandmother. One day the grandmother sensed her death near. She asked him to go to the river and get some water so she could be blessed before her death. He refused. This angered the grandmother so much. She cursed him and told him that he should never drink river water again. Soon after, she died.

Since then, the partridge boy found that he could not drink river water, or cross a river or bathe in a river. He tried once, and when he stepped into the water, the skin came off his feet. When he tried to drink, the skin came off his head and neck. But he needed water. So the only water he could get was dew, which he and his descendants still feed on. Even today, the skin of a partridge has conspicuous scars at the base of the feet and neck where the boy's skin came off.

10

The foolish Lion and Hare

Long ago Hare and Lion used to live together. They ate their food together and did everything together. Lion's mother lived under a small bush somewhere in the forest while Hare's mother lived in a hole in the ground. Hare and Lion used to give their mothers food all the time.

Once there was a great famine in the whole country. One day Hare suggested to his friend, "Why don't we kill our mothers? Then we can eat all the food we a get."

Lion was very stupid and greedy so he said that it was a good idea. They decided that minute to go and kill their mothers. When Lion got to the place where his mother lived he did not hesitate to kill her. Hare, however, did not kill his mother. He told her to go and hide in another place and he would bring her food every day. When they got home the Lion was very happy and told Hare that his mother was dead. Hare also pretended to be happy and said that he had killed his mother. They stayed together and ate all the food. Hare started the habit of keeping quiet in the evening and then all of a sudden answering, "Yes, what do you want?"

After listening for sometime he would answer, "V. C., wait for me. I am coming."

When Lion asked him who had called him, Hare answered, "My mother's ghosts are calling me." When Lion asked what they wanted, Hare answered, "The liver and the intestines." This was the favourite meat of Hare's mother.

Then Lion would tell him to hurry up and take the food to his mother's ghosts. Then Hare would pack the necessary food for his mother and leave in a hurry. This business went on for a long time until Lion became suspicious. Sometimes Hare would come home with his head clean shaven and when Lion asked him who had shaved his head, Hare would reply that he rubbed his head against a stone until all his hair came off.

One day when Hare prepared food to take to his mother, Lion decided to follow him. He discovered Hare's mother hidden in a cave. This annoyed Lion very, very much. He realized that Hare had fooled

After listening for sometime he would answer "V. C., wait for me. I am coming."

him. Lion was so angry with Hare that he decided to kill Hare's mother secretly. So one day when Hare was collecting some firewood, Lion went privately to the cave where Hare's mother had been hidden and killed her.

In the evening after the meal was ready, Hare said, "Yes, what do you want?" Then, after a pause, "V.C., wait for me, I am coming."

When Lion asked him what was happening he told the same story of the ghosts calling him and asking him to take the liver and the intestines.

This time Lion was quite amused and he helped Hare to pack the food as if nothing had happened. Hare left the house and as usual went to his mother's cave. You can imagine how horrified Hare was when he found that his mother had been killed. Hare was very miserable but he did not tell his friend Lion as he did not know for sure if Lion knew the secret his mother.

The poor miserable Hare went back home and no matter how hard he tried he could not stop the tears running from his eyes. Lion kept on asking Hare why tears were coming from his eyes and Hare said because it was very smoky. After sometime Lion asked him, "Is it because I killed your mother?"

Hare answered that was why he was crying and after that he cried freely for a long time.

Hare being clever wanted to make money out of everything. No sooner had he awakened the very next morning than he started thinking how to make use of his mother's body. He got up very early in the morning and went to his mother's cave. He took her dead body, washed it with a lot of perfume, dressed her with very smart clothes and carried her to the market place where he made her stand while leaning on a tree.

When Hare's mother died, her mouth was open and it remained open all the time. So when the people came to the market they looked at her and said, "Why is that woman standing in such a funny position with a smile on her face?" They could not understand at all. Hare was waiting at a distance to see what would happen to his mother.

After some time the son of the King came to the market. He was a very rough boy and when he saw Hare's mother smiling, he pushed her and said, "Go away, foolish woman. What makes you stand here smiling with that stupid smile?" He pushed the Hare's mother and the poor woman fell down. Hare was waiting for such a thing to happen. He came running to the King's son got hold of him and started crying, telling him, "You have killed my mother! You have killed my mother!"

All the people in the market came to see what was happening and they would have beaten the King's son to death for killing the poor old woman if the King had not arrived just at that time to tell the people to stop. He gave his sympathy to Hare and asked him what he wanted.

Hare said his mother could not be replaced by money or gold. He said that all he wanted was the King's daughter. The people were surprised to hear what Hare had chosen. The poor King had no alternative but to give Hare his daughter to take as his wife with sacks of gold, servants and all the other necessary things which the daughter of a king must have.

Hare, despite the fact that he had gained so much out of his mother's death, was not happy and wanted to punish Lion. So he went back to his old home and told Lion, "Thank you for killing my mother. I am sure you didn't know that the King of this country loves dead bodies and can spend any amount of money to buy them. Come to my house and see how much I got for my dead mother."

Lion regretted that he had not thought of selling his mother. After some time Lion decided to kill his two sisters, his brother and a cousin to sell them to the King and gain four times as much as Hare had. So Lion went and killed all his relatives and put them on the donkey's back. Lion walked to the King's palace. There he told the servants that he had something very precious which he wanted to sell to the King.

He did not tell them what it was and so they had to go and call the King to come. When the King came he asked Lion, "What do you want to sell to me?"

Lion uncovered the four dead bodies and said, "Here, you can give me as much money and gold as I want because I have got four very young beautiful dead bodies to sell to you." The King could not understand what Lion was talking about and asked him, "How did those poor young ones die?"

Lion was so stupid, he blurted out, "I killed them so as to get a lot of gold and other things from you."

Poor Lion did not know that he was in trouble until the King blew his whistle to call his soldiers and told them to beat Lion until he was dead. So Lion was killed and Hare was happy that he had avenged his mother's death and gained so much by his cunning.

11

Cinji, Kamau and Mwari

Once there was a very wealthy man, who lived near Chania River. He had one wife and two children a boy and a girl. The two children were well brought by their parents. The girl grew up to be a charming woman of startling beauty. The boy grew up very strong and intelligent. The two were happy together. When they became older, the boy would go with his father to look after the cattle. They had a large herd.

The girl stayed at home with her mother. She learned to cultivate and to do house work. She used to fetch water and firewood, and her mother taught her to manage the home. The whole family was hard working and they became very wealthy because there were only four of them to share the wealth.

As time went by, the parents became older and older, eventually, they came to the end of their lives. The mother died first and then the father. The two children mourned for days. They had loved their parents and were greatly saddened by their death.

Cinji, the boy, and his sister, Mwari, stayed together, working hard but enjoying what they gained. One day Mwari met a handsome young man who wooed her. She fell in love with him. He told her his name was Kamau. Mwari used to meet Kamau by the river and they had long conversations. One day, Kamau was invited home by Mwari. It turned out that Kamau was a friend of Cinji. They had met more than once during various ceremonies. From then on he used to visit the two in their home every evening.

One day, a group of young men met. Kamau was one of them. They planned to kill Cinji since he was so wealthy. The men did not know that Kamau was Mwari's lover.

On that same evening, Kamau went to Cinji's home and warned him. Kamau and Cinji decided that they would have to run away from the young men.

In the middle of the night, they took all their belongings and transferred them to the forest, where nobody was living. They came back for Mwari and the cattle. The three led their cattle into the middle of the forest.

For the first few months, they worked hard establishing a new home and preparing a shamba. The cattle grew fat because of the green forest grass. They stayed there for many years and no one ever appeared. They fenced the home and they were always armed with lances, spears, clubs and arrows, ready to attack any intruders.

When they were certain that they had been forgotten, Cinji and Kamau decided to go out to the nearby villages and attend the ceremonial dancing and songs, called Kibata. Before the two left, they taught Mwari a song which they would sing when they came back so that she would know she could open the door. She also learned what she should reply. After the ceremony, they would come and sing:

Cinji, Cinji I have come, Cinji,
Open for me, Cinji, with my friend, Cinji,
And my fighting implements, Cinji.

Mwari would reply,

Cinji, Cinji, let me open, Cinji,
Nothing's wrong, Cinji.

Either of them could add anything to the song, to explain if anything was wrong.

The two men took their weapons and went to the ceremonial dance. They enjoyed themselves and after the dance they came home. Cinji sang and his sister replied and opened the door. This went on for many days.

The men who had planned to kill Cinji had been very angry when they, learned that he had fled. They had sent three spies to find them. The spies had wandered all over the forest looking for Cinji, his sister and Kamau. After many months they found them. The spies did not dare attack at once but hung around for several days. They listened, and usually they saw Cinji and Kamau going out to the dance. They tried to break in as quietly as they could but they found the fence too sturdy for them.

Mwari was very alert and heard every noise. She heard the intruders, but she didn't think that anyone could have found their home. She thought it was just the wind. One night, she went and peeped through a tiny hole. She saw three poorly dressed men with long hair and rough skin. She knew they wouldn't be able to open the door and so she left them to do what they would.

When Cinji and Kamau approached, the men hid and listened to what the two sang. They learned to sing like Cinji. Mwari reported the event. Cinji and Kamau said that it was her imagination. The following few nights, Mwari saw the hairy men again and reported what she had seen but her reports were ignored.

A few nights later, the hairy men came and sang exactly like Cinji, lowering their voices. Mwari went and opened the gate for them. She was so frightened that she just stood rooted to the ground not knowing what to do. The men told her she could either go with them or be killed. She agreed to go with them.

The men were very hungry and asked to take some food with them. Mwari decided that since the food was ready, they could eat and then travel. The men ordered Mwari to leave the gates open, so that if Cinji and Kamau approached, they could easily run away. Mwari supplied the men with nice food. During the serving, Mwari kept on singing:

Cinji, Cinji, I told you Cinji,
More than once, Cinji,
That I was spied on, Cinji, by three men.
Cinji, Cinji, Cinji, hurry up,
Cinji with your spear, Cinji,
And your knife, Cinji.

She repeated the song getting louder and louder each time. As Cinji and Kamau approached, from the village they heard Mwari singing. They listened. They realized what had occurred. They hurried forward. Just when they were at the gate they saw

They hid by the fence, one on each side of the gate.

Mwari being dragged out by the three hairy men. They hid by the fence, one on each side of the gate. As the three men were passing, they took them by surprise and killed them.

After this incident the three young people continue to live in the forest. But they took greater care against intruders. They were happy but after some years, they grew homesick and wanted to see their friends again. Kamau was sent to their previous home. There, Kamau found that the conspirators had dispersed to their own homes and had forgotten their plot. Kamau reported this to Cinji and Mwari. They all decided that they must go back and live among their neighbours. They carried all their belongings with them plus very many cows and goats and a large stock of grain.

At home they occupied their former houses. Kamau's piece of land was now fertile with good, green grass. Kamau, Mwari and Cinji prepared a party for their neighbours. Everyone was happy and during that party, it was announced that Kamau was going to marry Mwari.

The marriage was very happy. Mwari retired to Kamau's home. Kamau and Cinji divided their property in half, but Cinji was given some cows as a dowry by Kamau. Mwari and Kamau lived happily and worked hard. Cinji also married. His wife was a beautiful girl, and made a wonderful wife. Cinji was very pleased with her and very happy for the rest of his days.

12

Kahuru the Crow

One day Wamabuku, the rabbit, decided to give a party. He invited all the other animals that had invited him before to similar parties. For the party Wamabuku had slaughtered many fat goats and cows. On the day of the party, Wamabuku got all his servants to decorate his house for the fiesta. All the animals arrived in rapid succession — Wamuthige, the hyena and his family, Wamacege, the porcupine, Kahuru, the crow and many others.

The animals ate the meat to their satisfaction. After the meal they began to dance. In the evening, the party was over and the animals prepared to leave. Wamuthige, the hyena and his family, being greedy animals, decided to get more meat from Wamabuku. Wamabuku was surprised at their greed and decided to teach them a lesson. Wamabuku told the hyena that only the "undesirable" fat meat was remaining. Since hyenas love fat meat their mouths became moist with saliva.

Wamabuku then sent his servants to the garden to collect all his young thriving gourds. The gourds were split into halves. The succulent white inside called "mego" was removed. Since it was exceedingly bitter, some liquid fat was poured over the mego. The hyenas were shown the melting mego. At the sight, the hyenas became panicky.

Wamuthige, after some thinking, called Kahuru. "Kahuru," he said, "please get a thread and needle. Then come and knit our back outlets tight so that when we have eaten all this melting meat, we shall not waste any. It is so sweet and we can't afford to have delicacies wasted."

Kahuru, being of a kind-hearted family, went to fetch a needle and thread. Meanwhile the hyenas ate nearly all the mego. When Kahuru returned with the needle and thread he was asked to start his operation on the hyenas.

The mego in the hyenas' stomachs had intermingled with the meat and other food. All the hyenas were suffering from flatulence. When Kahuru started, the hyenas began to get stouter and stouter due to the air in their stomachs. The hyenas brought their hindquarters as near to Kahuru as possible so that kahuru would not miss any.

When the hyenas were so swollen up that they could swell no more all their back openings burst with the pressure. All the stuff the hyenas had eaten was discharged from inside at a high velocity. Since Kahuru was busy on their backs, he suffered heavily. All the stuff from inside the hyenas, liquid and solid, was deposited on him. So much was put there, that he lay there covered all over and helpless. The hyenas left without helping Kahuru from his disgrace. Kahuru did not know what had happened and anyway, he was not to blame.

That night, rain fell in abundance and drenched the countryside. Kahuru was cleaned. He flew to the nearest tree and perched there. In the morning he found he could see and flew to his home.

A few weeks later Kahuru decided to give a feast especially for the hyenas. He notified Wamuthige, who collected all the hyenas. The party was to be in Kahuru's home. Kahuru was to carry all the hyenas up, since hyenas don't fly. Kahuru chose a spot where the hyenas would assemble, and told them to hold each other by the tail. Then Kahuru would take Wamuthige who would be in the front. Thus all the other hyenas would be pulled behind in a long string.

While they were waiting, the hyenas danced, singing:

We are going up high to eat fat, fat meat,
And when we say 'fat'
We mean meat purely white.

When Kahuru arrived and picked up the first hyena, all the others followed, still singing happily. When they had flown up many miles, Kahuru shouted at the last hyena, "Can you still see the ground?"

"Yes," was the reply. They flew on, still singing until they could see the ground no longer.

Then Kahuru told the hyenas to stop singing and make ready for "white" meat. Then all of a sudden, he let Wamuthige go, and through the air the hyenas dropped. Their fall was a great one. Kahuru flew down and, from a safe distance, jeered teasingly at the groaning, fractured cripples. Then he flew happily back to his home.

13

The last days of Wamugumo

Wamugumo told the children many more stories. Some were stories of his own and some were fables. However, Wamugumo grew older day by day. As he became older he became weaker. Soon he could no longer run after wild animals.

During the days of his old age, famine arose in the country. Wamugumo became very weak because he had nothing to eat. One day, he saw a donkey. He thought that it must be very fat. He longed for meat, especially for fat meat. So he killed the donkey which his neighbour possessed. He cooked the meat and ate it. He became very sick.

He became so sick that he was on the point of death and was taken to hospital. There he was given food and medicine and he started to get better again.

After repeated injections, Wamugumo started to show signs of regaining his health. Before, he had been unable to move his limbs and he breathed heavily. Conversation had become a herculean task for him. After the injections he started talking and moving his limbs. The doctor asked him questions, such as why he had dared to eat a donkey. Wamugumo answered them readily.

He told the doctor that he had stayed for many days without any meat.

"I remember," he told the doctor, "that when I was a very small boy, my father used to tell me stories while we were roasting meat. At that time he told me that when a man eats food, all the food later comes out, but when he eats meat, all the meat stays in his muscles. He told me that there was a man that lived near him at one time. That man ate nothing but food. He never ate meat. No food remained in his body for a long time, and though he looked healthy, he was very light. When he died, he was carried easily from his home by a small boy because he was as light as a feather.

"My father told me that he wanted me to be a strong man. He told me that I must eat as much meat as I can. Most of the things that my father told me have proved to be true and I feared that if I did not eat meat, I would be as light as a feather. The only meat that I can get now is that of tame animals since I am too old to hunt. The donkey came too near me and shouted. I frightened it and it did not move so I thought my god had sent me the donkey. It was easy meat, so I killed it."

He kept on talking to nurses and looking quite lively. The doctor told him that he would not die.

Wamugumo felt quite well but very hungry and giddy. At this time Wamugumo was still wearing animal skin clothes. The doctor told the nurses that Wamugumo smelt of many days sweat and should be washed and given clean clothes. Wamugumo protested, saying that he had never had a bath in his life and it would make him cold.

The nurses forced him since the doctor had ordered it. They washed him with hot water and soap, an experience that Wamugumo hated. Instead of giving Wamugumo back his skins, the nurses dressed Wamugumo in white hospital clothes. Wamugumo now looked very rich. He was cold in the clothes, and he was shivering much. He was put in bed and covered with blankets.

"What a place!" Wamugumo exclaimed. "I've never slept in a bed." He deserted the bed and belligerently asked for his skins back. The nurses feared him because they thought he was mad and although he was very old he was still strong. He was given his skins. He felt he was unable to walk home.

"I am going to die," he cried. "How can one possibly be expected to live after a bath and these strange queer garments?"

He refused all the medicines and became very wild. One nurse calmed him. He spread his skins under the bed and slept helplessly there. The nurse tried to take his temperature but he grabbed the thermometer and broke it.

"If I die" he said weakly, "I don't leave any curses to anyone."

The doctor tried to give him medicine but Wamugumo refused. The doctor tried to force the medicine through Wamugumo's clenched teeth. Wamugumo fell back. That night his condition grew steadily worse. In the morning, he died.

www.ingramcontent.com/pod-product-compliance
Lightning Source LLC
LaVergne TN
LVHW051041070526
838201LV00067B/4881